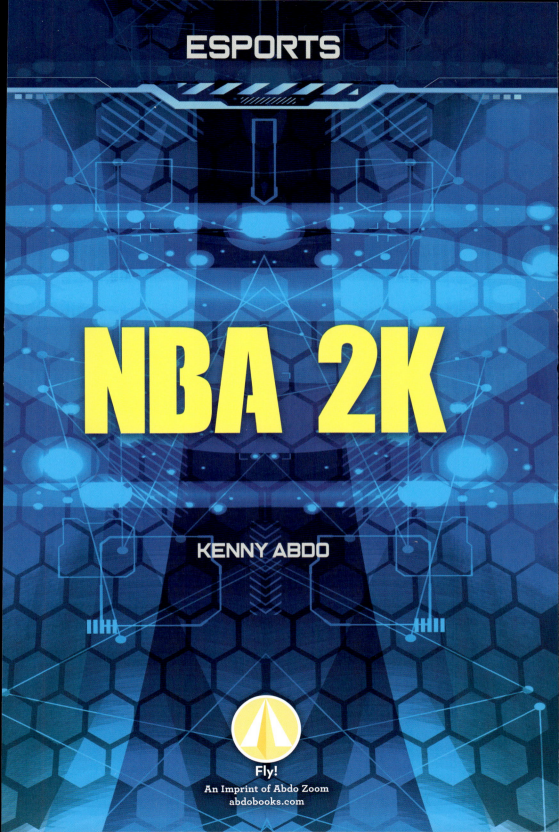

abdobooks.com

Published by Abdo Zoom, a division of ABDO, P.O. Box 398166, Minneapolis, Minnesota 55439. Copyright © 2023 by Abdo Consulting Group, Inc. International copyrights reserved in all countries. No part of this book may be reproduced in any form without written permission from the publisher. Fly!™ is a trademark and logo of Abdo Zoom.

Printed in the United States of America, North Mankato, Minnesota.
052022
092022

THIS BOOK CONTAINS RECYCLED MATERIALS

Photo Credits: Alamy, AP Images, Getty Images, Shutterstock, ©Tampamann p.16 / CC BY-SA 4.0
Production Contributors: Kenny Abdo, Jennie Forsberg, Grace Hansen
Design Contributors: Candice Keimig, Neil Klinepier

Library of Congress Control Number: 2021950295

Publisher's Cataloging-in-Publication Data

Names: Abdo, Kenny, author.
Title: NBA 2K / by Kenny Abdo.
Description: Minneapolis, Minnesota : Abdo Zoom, 2023 | Series: Esports | Includes online resources and index.
Identifiers: ISBN 9781098228491 (lib. bdg.) | ISBN 9781644947852 (pbk.) | ISBN 9781098229337 (ebook) | ISBN 9781098229757 (Read-to-Me ebook)
Subjects: LCSH: Video games--Juvenile literature. | eSports (Contests)--Juvenile literature. | NBA 2K (Game)--Juvenile literature. | 2K Sports (Firm)--Juvenile literature. | Basketball--Juvenile literature.
Classification: DDC 794.8--dc23

TABLE OF CONTENTS

NBA 2K 4

Backstory 8

Journey 14

Glossary 22

Online Resources 23

Index 24

NBA 2K

Debuting in 1999, *NBA 2K* has been the number one basketball video game ever since.

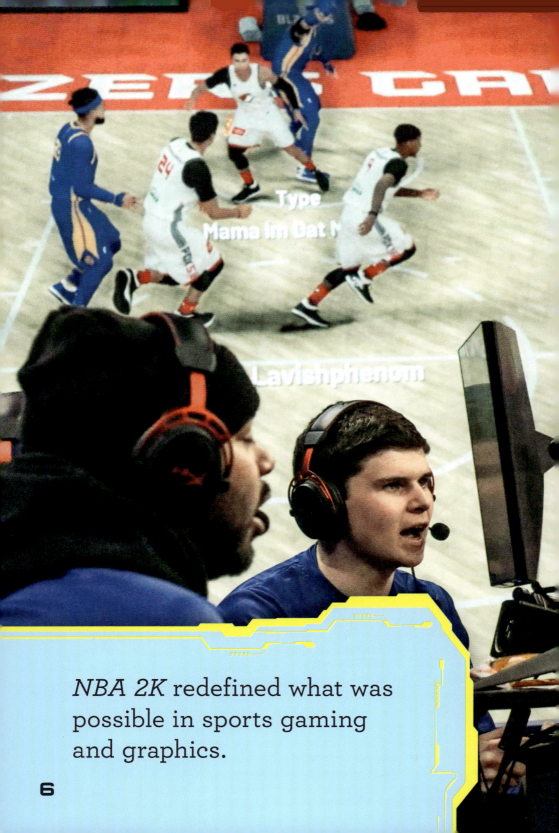

NBA 2K redefined what was possible in sports gaming and graphics.

The game lets players come together as a team in the exciting world of esports!

BACKSTORY

Video game giant Sega needed a sports game for its systems. However, the creators of the popular *Madden NFL* series, Electronic Arts (EA), did not want to work with Sega.

Sega reached out to game maker Visual Concepts to help. *NBA 2K* was released in 1999. It was only available for the Sega Dreamcast. In 2000, *2K1* was released.

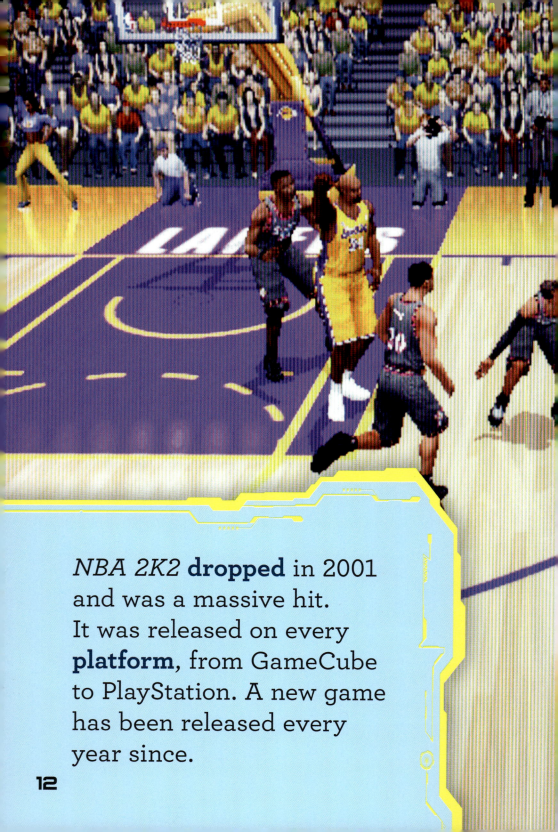

NBA 2K2 **dropped** in 2001 and was a massive hit. It was released on every **platform**, from GameCube to PlayStation. A new game has been released every year since.

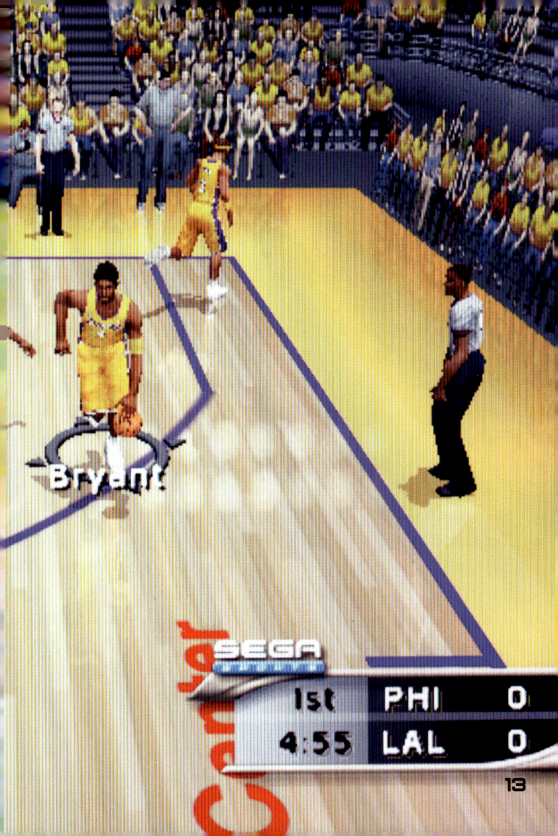

JOURNEY

With the arrival of online gaming, the *2K* series became popular worldwide. The NBA and Take-Two Interactive created the NBA 2K **League**, a professional esports competition.

The NBA 2K **League's** first **season** began in 2018. Each of the 17 groups played as a different NBA team. The Knicks Gaming won the first league **championship**!

The **league** expanded to 24 teams. T-Wolves Gaming were crowned the champions of the 2019 NBA 2K League after defeating 76ers GC, netting the $360,000 prize!

In 2020, Wizards District Gaming won the **season** 3 title! They took down the Warriors Gaming Squad, bringing home $420,000 in prize money!

Wizards District Gaming **clinched** the victory again in 2021. By defeating Jazz Gaming, they became the first team in the **league's** history with back-to-back **championships**!

Many NBA teams and former players see big things for the future esports. They continue to invest in esports **franchises** and events.

NBA 2K has evolved into much more than a basketball video game. Each year, the NBA 2K **League dominates** the world of esports, gaining a roster of fans and players alike.

GLOSSARY

championship – a game held to find a first-place winner.

clinch – to confirm a win.

dominate – to be more important or powerful than others.

drop – when something that is highly anticipated is released to the public.

league – a group of teams that compete against each other.

platform – a type of video game console.

season – the portion of the year when certain games are played.

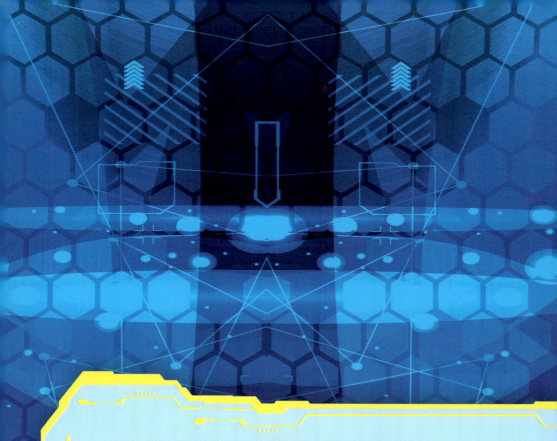

ONLINE RESOURCES

To learn more about NBA 2K, please visit **abdobooklinks.com** or scan this QR code. These links are routinely monitored and updated to provide the most current information available.

INDEX

76ers GC (team) 16

championships 15

EA (developer) 8

Jazz Gaming (team) 18

Knicks Gaming (team) 15

Madden NFL (game) 8

National Basketball Association (NBA) 20

NBA 2K (game) 6, 10, 21

NBA 2K1 (game) 10

NBA 2K2 (game) 12

Sega 8, 10

T-Wolves Gaming (team) 16

Take-Two Interactive (publisher) 14

Visual Concepts (developer) 10

Warriors Gaming Squad (team) 17

Wizards District Gaming (team) 17, 18